Weekly Reader Books presents

BERNARD
OF SCOTLAND YARD

by Berniece Freschet

Pictures by Gina Freschet

CHARLES SCRIBNER'S SONS • NEW YORK

Text copyright © 1978 Berniece Freschet
Illustrations copyright © 1978 Gina Freschet

Library of Congress Cataloging in Publication Data
Freschet, Berniece.
Bernard of Scotland Yard.
SUMMARY: An enterprising Bostonian mouse assists
his cousin, a Scotland Yard inspector, in
apprehending a gang of jewel thieves.
[1. Mice —Fiction.   2.   Robbers and outlaws—
Fiction]   I. Freschet, Gina.   II. Title.
PZ7.F88968Bd   [E]   78-9584
ISBN 0-684-15931-7

Printed in the United States of America

For Frank,
son and brother,
with love

AUNT HILLY'S VISIT

Bernard lived in an old brownstone house
at the top of Beacon Hill in Boston,
Massachusetts. He lived in the house
with his father and mother, and his three
sisters, and two brothers. Bernard's
grandparents had lived in this house.
And so had his great-grandparents.

From the outside the old brownstone
looked just as it always had looked.
But inside—
things were happening.

From the moment they had gotten
the news of Great-Aunt Hilly's visit,
the family's easy, comfortable way
of life had changed.

First the house was swept,
...and dusted
...and mopped.
Then the best china was brought out—
tablecloths and curtains were starched
and ironed—
everyone helped.

Father climbed up to
the chandelier and carefully
cleaned every glass crystal.

Bernard's sisters wiped the
mouseprints from the
walls, while his brothers rubbed
lemon oil on each rail of
the oak staircase.

His mother gave Bernard the important job
of polishing the big old silver teapot,
which had been in the family for years.

While everyone was busy cleaning, Bernard's
mother spent her time in the kitchen baking.
What delicious smells filled the house—
    cinnamon tea cakes and walnut tarts,
    steamed puddings and butter biscuits,
    and flaky pork pies.
It was almost more than one could bear.

Finally the big day arrived. Everything was ready.

Just as the hall clock chimed four chimes,
Aunt Hilly swept through the doorway.
She looked exactly as Bernard had pictured
an English Lady would look. She wore a
velvet dress and lacy gloves.
A large flowered hat made her look even
taller than she was, which was considerably
tall indeed. Aunt Hilly was a most
impressive-looking lady.

Bernard and his brothers bowed politely—
his sisters curtseyed.

"My, what a perfectly beautiful table,"
said Aunt Hilly. "This is every bit as
nice as our annual Ladies' Garden Tea."

While they had tea, Aunt Hilly told them news
about relatives. Bernard didn't pay much attention
until he heard Aunt Hilly say, "You know,
don't you, that my son Foster is an
Inspector with Scotland Yard?"

Bernard's ears twitched.

He brushed the cake crumbs from his whiskers
and turned to hear more. His cousin an
Inspector at Scotland Yard?
How fascinating!

"Right now Foster is at work on a most
baffling case. He's after a gang of jewel
thieves. They steal diamonds, but only
diamonds of a certain size—most puzzling.
But there now, that's enough about relatives
in England. Do tell me all about your
lovely family and life here in America."

When Aunt Hilly heard of Bernard's
many adventures, she looked impressed.
"How exciting. You mean that Bernard
took a rocket to the moon? *Fancy that!*"
Bernard tried to look important, but it was
difficult with a mouthful of biscuit and honey.

Aunt Hilly looked through her eyeglasses.
"But why didn't you stop and see us?
Foster would have been delighted to meet you."

Aunt Hilly tapped the glasses against her chin.
"Such a bright young mouse, you could have
helped him with his work, such as that case
he's working on now—positively baffling."
It took Bernard just ten seconds to decide.
That's exactly what he would do—*visit Cousin Foster.*

"I'll leave tomorrow," he said.
But...how was he to get all the way to London, England?

TO LONDON, TO LONDON

"That's the answer—a balloon is
just the thing. I wish I had read
this book before my last trip," said
Bernard. "And I know just how to make
it—if I work through the night, I
can leave before noon."

He jumped down and hurried
through the house—
gathering things as he went.
He took a birthday candle from
his sisters' room, and two of
his brothers' biggest balloons.

In the kitchen of the big house
he found two bottle caps,
some string, and a strawberry basket
with a strawberry stuck in the corner...
which he ate.

In the big bedroom he found a hairnet and six
brass buttons. He put everything together in
the attic, and was soon hard at work.

By morning, Bernard had finished.

Everyone helped carry

the balloons up to the roof. He lighted

the candle and filled them with hot air.

"Stand back," cried Bernard, untying the mooring string.

And with a wave of his hand—and a gasp from his mother—Bernard took off...up into the sky.

Dodging chimneys, the balloon floated
above the roof tops. It swept over the
harbor and across the tip of Cape Cod.
A westerly wind caught the balloon and
it sailed away on a current of warm air...
out over the Atlantic Ocean.

"How *v-a-s-t*," said Bernard.

Days passed.
Below and all around him splashed
ocean waves. "I do hope I'm on course.

If my calculations are right, I should
sight land tomorrow."

But the next morning Bernard couldn't even see
to the other side of his basket.
Fog swirled all around. "I don't know
if I'm over land or water," he said.

Just as Bernard was beginning to get
really worried, the fog began to lift.
He saw a gray stone tower poking up
through the mist. "The Tower of London!"
cried Bernard. As the fog cleared, other
landmarks came into view. "There's
Westminister Abbey—and Big Ben—and
Buckingham Palace. Hurrah! Hurrah!
I made it to London."

"Good for me!" shouted Bernard.

Bernard threw out the anchor. He landed
right in the middle of Trafalgar Square.
After getting directions from
a friendly bobby, he was soon riding
on top of a double-decker bus on his
way to Scotland Yard.

"Inspector Foster is out, but you can wait in his office," said the clerk.

Bernard was impressed. From the pictures and newspaper stories on the walls, he saw that Inspector Foster had solved a number of dangerous cases. "What an exciting life. I do hope Cousin Foster will let me help," Bernard thought.

The door opened and in stepped a figure
wearing a bowler hat and an overcoat.
"Hello," said Bernard, "I'm your cousin from Boston."

"Bernard? By Jove—what a jolly surprise.
I'm only sorry I won't be able to show you
the sights—you see, I'm right in the
middle of a most difficult case."

"Yes, I know," said Bernard. "In fact,
   that's why I'm here, to see if I can help."

"A splendid idea," said Foster. "But are you up to it?
   Dangerous business, you know."

But after Bernard told of some of his adventures, Foster
agreed that he was certainly up to it. "We'll make you
a temporary Inspector," he said. They went
downstairs, where Bernard was outfitted. When he saw
himself in the mirror, Bernard not only looked like a full-fledged
Inspector of Scotland Yard—he began to feel like one.

"Let's go home for tea and I'll fill you
   in on the case," said Foster. Over cups
   of hot tea and biscuits with marmalade,
   Foster told Bernard about the jewel robberies.

"We're certain it's the work of the Mole Gang,
but it's impossible to track them down—
they live in the drain pipes under the city. What
we can't figure out is why they steal only
diamonds of a certain size," said Foster, scratching
an ear and frowning. "We have a tip that the gang
is going to be at Lady Thistlethwaite's masked ball
tonight. It's one of the biggest parties of the year."

"And the ladies will be wearing their
most expensive jewelry," guessed Bernard.

"Right," nodded Foster. "There will be guards, but the Mole Gang is a cheeky bunch, and their leader, Rotter, is a most bold and cunning rascal. It will be dangerous, but you're welcome to come along if you want to risk it."

Of course Bernard was eager to go. That night, dressed in their costumes, Inspector Foster and Inspector Bernard arrived at Lady Thistlethwaite's house. The ballroom glittered with fancy costumes and sparkling jewels. *"How magnificent,"* said Bernard. For a moment he forgot he was on a dangerous case, but Foster reminded him.

"We'll mingle with the guests—keep your eyes open. If you see anything suspicious, give me a call."

Bernard mingled—even waltzing once around the ballroom with a very pretty "Maid Marian." Bernard was taking her a glass of punch when he heard a scream. "My necklace—it's gone! Oooh—." Lady Thistlethwaite swooned, knocking over a stack of plates, which fell, crashing to the floor.

All around the ballroom ladies clutched
their throats, shrieking, "My jewels,
they've been stolen!" Some even fell to the
floor in a faint.

Someone bumped into Bernard. His cup
flew out of his hand. He turned and
looked into the squinty eyes of a pirate.
"Blimey—sorry, mate, didn't see ya there."
Three other pirates joined him. "Let's
get going," called a raspy voice.
"Right behind you, Rotter." The pirates
quickly disappeared into the crowd.

"They must be the Mole Gang!" said
Bernard. He hurried after them,
forgetting all about Foster's
warning to call.

THE MOLE GANG

Bernard followed the pirates outside.
He saw the scurrying figures under the
corner street lamp, and then suddenly—
they disappeared.

"The only place they could have gone
is down the drain pipe," he said.
Carefully, Bernard slipped through
the grate, dropping to the pipe below.

The walls smelled damp and musty. He had expected to drop into blackness, but was surprised to see a glow coming from one of the tunnels.

He crept forward. As he got closer, Bernard saw that the glowing light came from a cluster of diamonds overhead, cleverly placed to catch and reflect the light from the street lamp above. "How ingenious! So that's what they do with the stolen diamonds." Bernard heard voices and moved closer.

The pirates were huddled around a table.
"Well, we pulled it off—and right under
Scotland Yard's nose," laughed the pirate
with the raspy voice.

"Yeah, Boss, but did we get enough
diamonds to finish our tunnel?"

"We'd better have," said Rotter. "Those
Scotland Yard Inspectors are getting
closer and closer. I'd rather not pull
another job for a while." Rotter threw
his sack on the table. "Empty out your
bags, boys, and let's have a look."
Jewels spilled out, flashing across the table.

Rotter frowned. "All right, who's the
wise guy who took the ruby bracelet
and the emerald necklace?"

"Guess it was me, Boss, who took the ruby
bracelet," a meek voice spoke.

"And I guess I'm the one who took the
emerald necklace," another voice croaked.

"Bobo?—Albert?—What's the big idea?"
hollered Rotter. "You
know we only use diamonds."

Bobo squinted up at Rotter. "It's
hard enough for us moles to see without
having to wear these dumb masks," he said.

"Yeah, Boss, he's right," agreed Albert,
stumbling over Bobo's foot.

"Aw, forget it," said Rotter. "Let's go
and see if we got enough diamonds this time
to finish lighting the main tunnel."
The gang scurried off.

No one saw the shadowy figure that
followed a short way behind.

"What rotten luck," said Rotter. "It looks like we'll have to pull one more job. It will be risky, but I think I know where we can heist all the diamonds we'll need."

Rotter lowered his voice. "Gather 'round boys and I'll tell you my plan."

Bernard moved closer, his ears straining to hear the hushed voices.

"You don't mean it, Boss," said Albert and Bobo together, their voices squeaking in disbelief. *"Not the Crown Jewels!"*

"Quiet," said Rotter. "You want to tell the whole world? No one will ever guess that we'd try for the 'Big Ones.' Now, here's how we'll pull it off."

"Surely you don't mean *The Crown Jewels!*" Foster said in stunned amazement.
Bernard nodded.
"I'm afraid so.

I couldn't hear how they were planning to do it, but they're going to make the heist tonight," said Bernard, feeling rather proud of the new word he'd learned at the moles' hideout.

"Astonishing," said Foster. "What a cheeky bunch—didn't I tell you that Rotter was a bold and cunning fellow? But thanks to you, Bernard, we'll be waiting for the beggars."

From his hiding place, crouched behind
a stone pillar in the Tower of London
(where the Crown Jewels were kept),
Bernard heard Big Ben strike twelve—*Gong!*
Midnight—then all was quiet. He peered
into the darkness, straining for some
sight or sound of the Mole Gang
—but there was nothing.

A faint scratching noise came from the walls
—or was it the floor?—maybe the ceiling?

Then Bernard saw shadowy figures that suddenly seemed to appear out of nowhere. The Mole Gang had arrived, digging their way in through a tunnel. Quickly they began to fill their sacks with jewels.

Foster gave a shrill blast on his whistle.
Guards came running! Figures scrambled
in every direction—shouting—shoving.
There was a scuffle—the Moles were not
going to give up without a fight.

Bernard grabbed a figure. "Blimey, mate, let go—*let go!*" hollered Bobo, with legs kicking and arms thrashing.

But Bernard held on tight.

"I've got him—I've got Rotter!" shouted Foster. For a
second Foster did have hold of Rotter, but Rotter bopped him with
his sack and Foster was left holding onto his own head.

In an instant Rotter disappeared, squeezing
himself under a door to make his getaway.

The Mole Gang was finally rounded up
(all except for Rotter, that is) and
taken off to Scotland Yard.

Much later, in front of a warm fireplace,
Bernard and Foster sipped hot mugs of cocoa.
"That Rotter is sure a slippery one," said
Foster, putting an ice bag on the large
purple lump on his forehead.

"That's a tough gang, all right," said
Bernard, patting a minute steak on
his bruised eye.

"Not a bad night's work," said Foster,
"even if Rotter did get away. But we'll
catch that rascal yet—his luck can't
last forever."

"I must say," said Bernard, leaning
back in his chair, "this was one
of the most exciting days in my life
—but how exhausting."

The telephone rang. When Foster returned,
excitement sounded in his voice. "I've
got great news, Bernard. Tomorrow, we're
invited to visit the Queen." But Bernard
didn't hear—he was fast asleep.

"Kneel," said the Queen.
"For your outstanding and splendid
efforts in saving the Crown Jewels,
I hereby knight you—Sir Foster—
Sir Bernard."

And then the Queen hung
a medal around each of their necks.
It was a grand ceremony.

Afterwards, the heroes were toasted.

"Hip—hip—hip—hooray!"
"Hip—hip—hip—hooray!"

WANTED
THE
MOLE GANG

A pretty miss came up to Bernard, and in
a voice as smooth as cream she said,
"Oh, Sir Bernard, how terribly brave
you are."

"Why, thank you, Miss…Miss…?"
"Oh, you may call me 'Maid Marian,'"
she said with a shy smile.
Her voice filled with admiration.
"Catching all those nasty criminals,"
she said as she took Bernard's arm.
"How very derring-do."

"How de*light*ful," said Bernard.